I'm Reading About

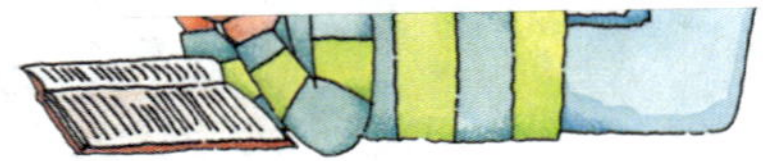

COLORADO

The Centennial State!

GALLOPADE

by Carole Marsh

Printed and Manufactured in Peachtree City, GA., USA
www.gallopade.com

Book design: John Hanson

Editorial manager: Janice Baker

Colorado is a great state.

It is one of a kind.

What makes Colorado special?

Let's read about it

and see!

NATIVE AMERICANS

Who lived in Colorado first?

Native Americans did!

They moved around to find food.
They hunted in Colorado's woods.
They fished in Colorado's rivers.
They gathered fruits and seeds and nuts.

EXPLORERS

The first explorers came to Colorado in 1706.
They came from the country of Spain.

Juan de Ulibarri was their leader.
He and his men were looking for new land!

HISTORY

In the 1850s, men found gold in Colorado.
Other people rushed to Colorado.
They wanted to find gold, too!
That period of time is called the
"Colorado Gold Rush."

Miners found silver in
Colorado, too.

Gold Rush

STATEHOOD

Colorado was the 38th state
to join the United States of America!

Isn't it great,
to be a state!
I bet Colorado
could hardly wait!

Colorado became a state in 1876.

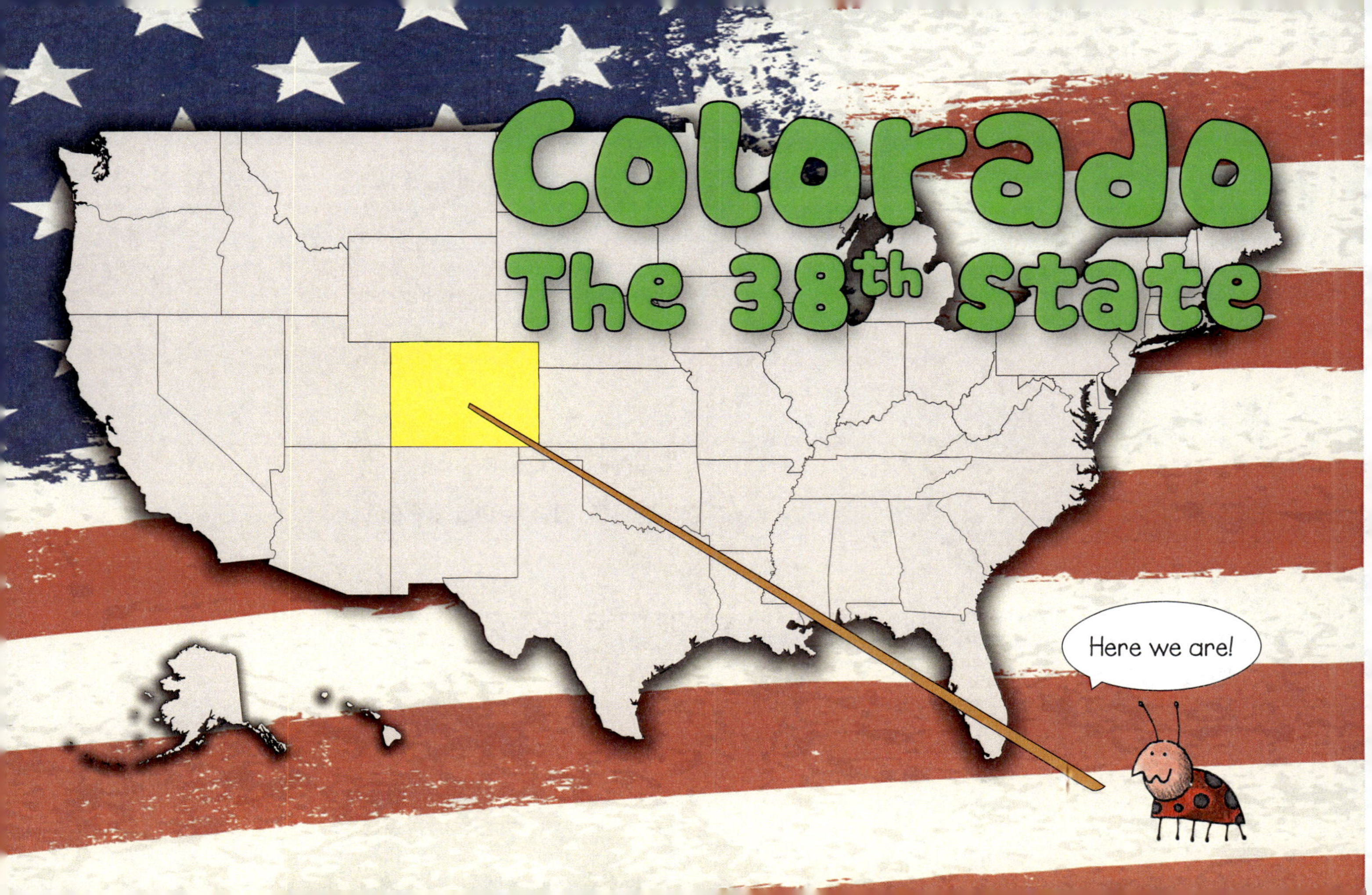
Colorado
The 38th State
Here we are!

FLAG

I am the state flag.
I was adopted in 1911.

What colors am I?
Red. White. Blue. Gold.

Look at me.
What else do you see?

I fly high over the state of Colorado!

CAPITAL

Say hello to Denver,
the capital city of Colorado!

There is an important building in Denver.
It is the State Capitol.
Colorado's laws are made there!

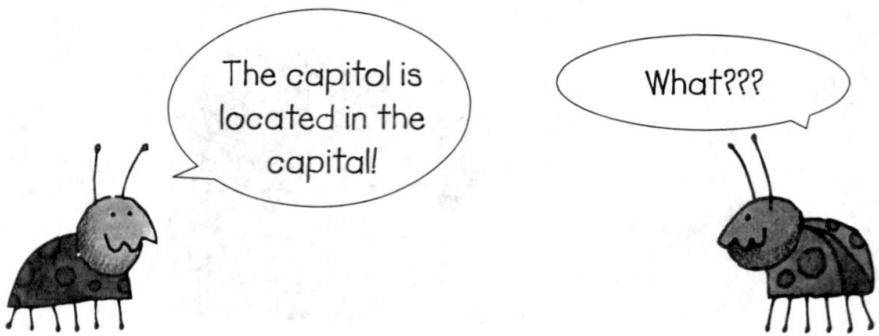

Capitol
Denver
Capital

SEAL

I am a seal,
but I am not the State Seal.
If I were, I would be very important.
I would be stamped on many official papers.
(Ouch, that might hurt!)

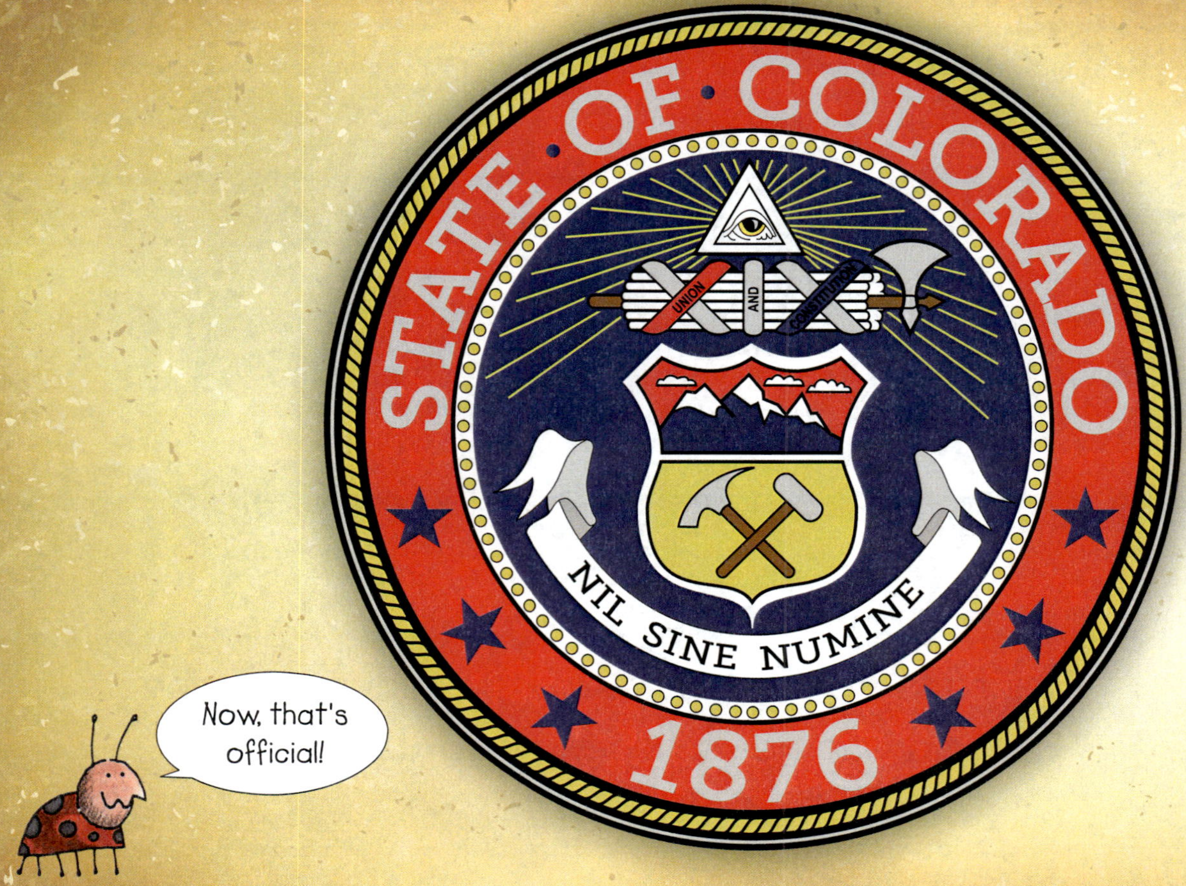
STATE OF COLORADO
UNION
AND
CONSTITUTION
NIL SINE NUMINE
1876
Now, that's official!

NICKNAME

State nicknames are fun!
State nicknames are great!
They share fun facts
about each state!

Colorado's nickname is "The Centennial State."

A "centennial" marks a period of 100 years. Colorado became a state 100 years after the Declaration of Independence was signed.

The Centennial State

BORDERS

Look at Colorado.
Colorado is in a region called "the Southwest."

Colorado borders seven other states.
Find them on the map!

Borders

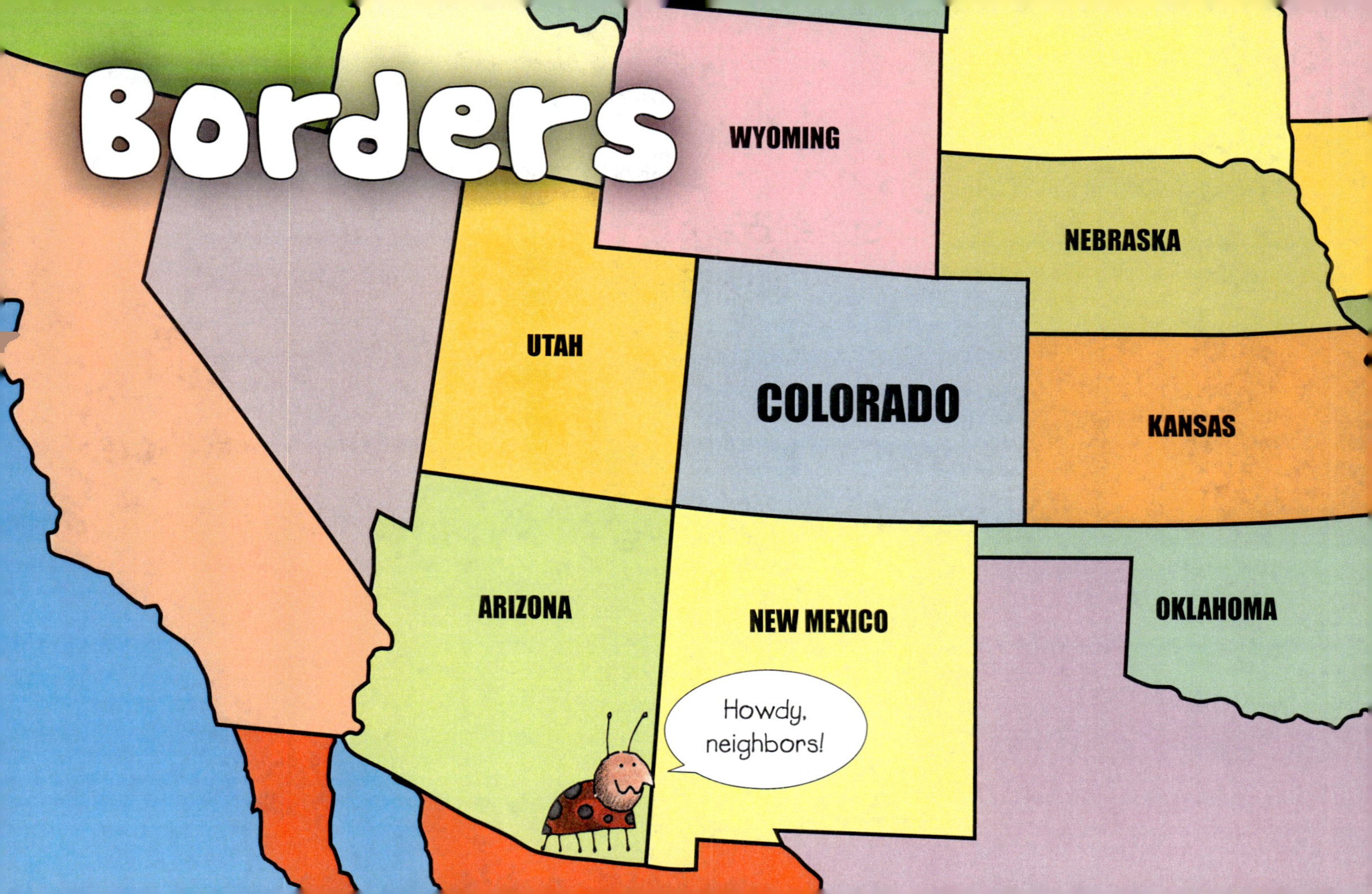
WYOMING
NEBRASKA
UTAH
COLORADO
KANSAS
ARIZONA
NEW MEXICO
OKLAHOMA
Howdy, neighbors!

COUNTIES

Colorado is divided into 64 counties.
Counties are a form of local government.
Counties provide services that people need!
Those services include:

Schools **Parks** **Libraries** **Police**
Firefighters **and More!**

Counties

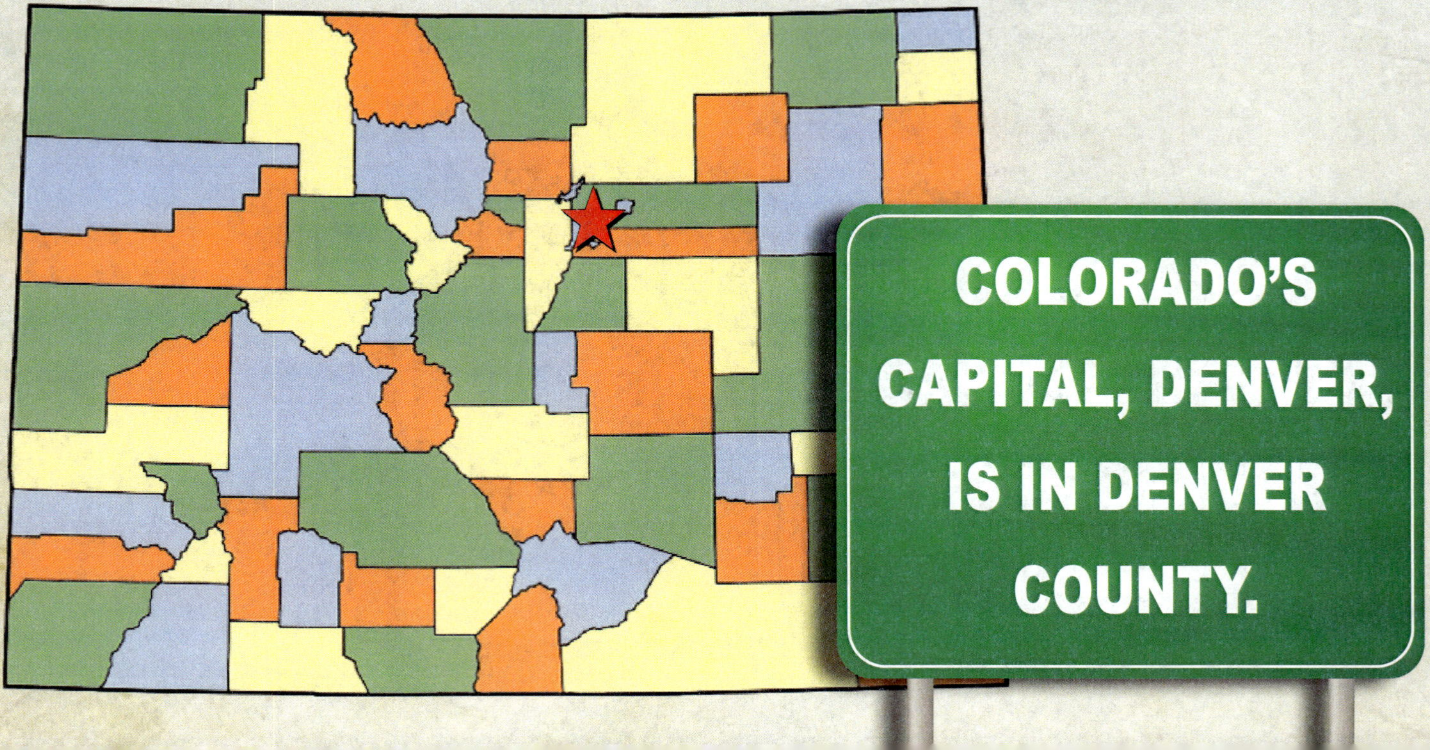

Many famous people

Chief Ouray
Chief of the Ute tribe

Mamie Eisenhower
First Lady and wife of President Dwight Eisenhower

Ruth Handler
Created the Barbie doll

call our state home!

Byron White
U.S. Supreme Court Justice

Scott Carpenter
One of the original seven U.S. astronauts

John Kerry
U.S. Secretary of State under President Barack Obama

Lark Bunting

BIRD

I am the state bird, and I fly
over Colorado, proud and high.

As I fly, up in the sky,
I flap my wings to tell you "Hi!"

The Colorado state bird is the Lark Bunting.

White and Lavender Columbine

FLOWER

I am the White and Lavender Columbine.
I am the state flower.

I grow where it's mild and sunny.
I bloom in summer.
I help make Colorado beautiful!

Look at me! Smell me!
I only grow in the
Rocky Mountains of Colorado.

Colorado Blue Spruce

TREE

I am a Colorado Blue Spruce—I'm the state tree.
All over Colorado's mountains is where to find me.

My roots run deep, they keep me strong.
My leaves stay green, all year long.

I stand up straight, big and tall.
Don't climb too high—it would hurt to fall!

Colorado Hairstreak Butterfly

I am the Colorado Hairstreak Butterfly.
I am the state insect.

I flit and I fly from flower to flower.
I am looking for nectar to drink.

Look at my beautiful wings.
What colors do you see?

INSECT

Rivers

RIVERS

Colorado has many rivers.
The Colorado River is the most important one.
It flows through seven U.S. states!

Colorado's rivers are home to many animals:

Birds **Beavers** **Snakes** **Fish** **Frogs** **and More!**

Rocky Mountains

Colorado's Rocky Mountains are the place to be.
Hiking, fishing, camping—
fun for you and me.

Winter weather brings lots of snow.
Temperatures drop to freezing and below!

MOUNTAINS

Great Plains

GREAT PLAINS

Eastern Colorado is part of the Great Plains.
The Great Plains are flat lands with tall grass.

This habitat is home to many animals:

Prairie Dogs **Bison** **Foxes** **Birds** **Gophers** **and More!**

The Great Plains stretch all the way up to Canada!

Garden of the Gods

LANDMARK

The Garden of the Gods is a group of rocks.
The red rocks are all different shapes and sizes.
Some of the rocks are tall.
Some are balanced on top of each other!

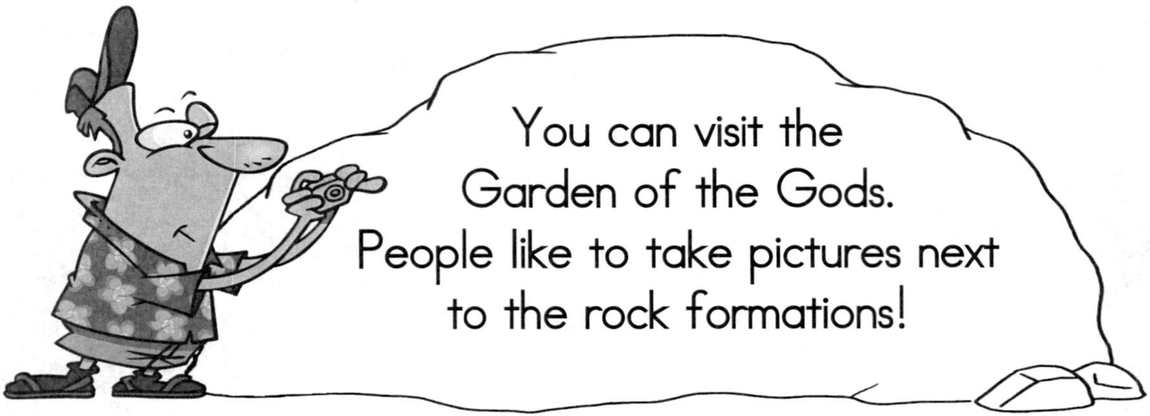

You can visit the
Garden of the Gods.
People like to take pictures next
to the rock formations!

Colorado Crops

AGRICULTURE

Colorado has many farms.
Why?
Because Colorado has good soil and a mild climate!

Some of the top crops grown in Colorado are:

Hay **Corn** **Wheat** **Potatoes**

Sports in Colorado

Baseball! Basketball! Football!
Colorado has it all.

Whether you like to watch or play,
You are sure to have a ball!

Avalanche **Rockies** **Broncos**

Nuggets **Buffaloes**

Rams

& More!

SPORTS

Colorado: Home of Snow Skiing

CLAIM TO FAME

Colorado is known for its ski slopes!
Many people travel to Colorado every winter.
They want to ski and snowboard.

Denver is known as the "Mile High City."

GLOSSARY

astronaut: a person trained to travel in space

climate: weather conditions in an area over a long period of time

Declaration of Independence: document that declared that the 13 American colonies were breaking free from Great Britain

elevation: height of a place above the ground

habitat: a place where plants or animals naturally live

laws: rules made by the government

nectar: a sweet liquid produced by plants, especially flowers

region: an area that has similar characteristics